Chloe's

RIVER RESCUE

SaMaNTHa TURNBULL

ILLUSTRaTeD bY

SaRaH DaVIS

ALLEN&UNWIN

SYDNEY · MELBOURNE · AUCKLAND · LONDON

Allen & Unwin
83 Alexander Street
Crows Nest NSW 2065
Australia
Phone: (61 2) 8425 0100
Email: info@allenandunwin.com
Web: www.allenandunwin.com

A Cataloguing-in-Publication entry is available from the
National Library of Australia
www.trove.nla.gov.au

ISBN 978 1 74331 987 1

Cover and text design by Vida & Luke Kelly
Set in 13pt Fairfield LT Std, Light
This book was printed in March 2015 at McPherson's Printing
Group, 76 Nelson St, Maryborough, Victoria 3465, Australia.

www.mcphersonsprinting.com.au

3 5 7 9 10 8 6 4 2

For Babs, Bob, Gem
and all anti-princess mums

CHAPTER  ONE

Grace goes cross-eyed as she spots the blue tentacle hanging down her forehead.

'I don't want to alarm you,' I say, 'but that's a Portuguese man-of-war. Don't touch it.'

Grace drops her surfboard. 'You mean a jellyfish?'

'It's often mistaken for a jellyfish, but it's actually a different class of ocean critter,' I say. 'A jellyfish is a single organism, while a Portuguese man-of-war is a siphonophore, which is a colony of very small predatory marine creatures.'

'Chloe Karalis, save the biological explanation!'

Grace yells. 'What is on my head?!'

I'm a scientist, so I often get the common names for different species mixed up with the scientific titles. 'Its proper name is a *physalia physalis*, but they're sometimes called... ummm...bluebottles. There's a bluebottle in your hair.'

Grace freezes. 'Should we run to the lifeguard?'

Grace Bennett is the fastest runner I know, but any sharp movement could result in a severe sting. And by the time I got to the lifeguard station and back, Grace's scalp could be burning from multiple stings.

'We can do it ourselves,' I say. 'We don't need rescuing.'

Grace manages a brave half-smile at the mention of our club motto. We're founding members of the Anti-Princess Club. We can solve our own problems, unlike the damsels in distress you read about in fairytales, which we actually call *unfairy*tales.

'Hurry, Chloe,' Grace whimpers. 'I think it's moving.'

I wish the other founding members, Emily Martin and Bella Singh, were here right now. Today, however, it's just me and Grace. I wanted to come to the beach to collect some molluscs for an aquarium I'm building, and Grace never passes up a chance to hit the waves.

'Let's do it,' I say. 'Bend down.'

I push my glasses up the bridge of my nose and carefully part a few strands of Grace's short blonde hair. There are tentacles everywhere. 'I'd love some tweezers and gloves,' I say. 'But fingers will have to do.'

I brace myself. There are up to three thousand touch receptors in each fingertip, so this could really hurt.

I delicately pinch the first tentacle and wince. It feels as if tiny electrified razor blades are lashing against my skin.

'Are you okay?' Grace asks.

I clench my teeth. 'It's not so bad,' I lie as I draw the tentacles through Grace's hair, untangling piece by slimy piece.

'Aaaaah!' Grace squeals. 'It got me on the ear!'

I spy the cone-shaped top of the bluebottle at the nape of her neck. 'I see the float,' I say. 'It's like the head. There's no venom in it, so I'm just going to grab it, okay?'

I pull off the bluebottle in a single swoop and throw it on the sand.

Grace is clutching her ear and I'm shaking my thumb and index finger.

'Thanks, Chloe. Not many people would touch a bluebottle with their bare hands like that.'

I swoosh my hand around in some saltwater then splash a little on the red welt on Grace's earlobe.

'Don't we need some vinegar?' she asks. 'Isn't that what takes the pain away?'

I remember reading about this. Doctors used to treat bluebottle stings with vinegar, but discovered it only works for super poisonous gelatinous zooplankton, like the deadly box jellyfish. 'No,' I say. 'We need to find some hot water – it will help ease the burn.'

Grace makes a run for a toilet block in the distance. I take off after her as she slows her stride to keep pace with me. We reach the girls' bathrooms and Grace turns on the shower taps full pelt. I stick my hand in the hot stream of water.

'That feels better already,' I say.

Grace doesn't hear. Her head is tilted sideways, her ear under the water. 'You know, sometimes I think of shaving off all of my hair because I hate brushing it every day,' she shouts. 'But it's finally come in handy for something.'

It's a sound hypothesis: if Grace were bald, she'd have a much sorer head right now. I don't think anyone would be willing to test the theory, though, even in the name of science.

CHAPTER TWO

A pair of feet in pink runners is sticking out from underneath Bella's dad's sports car.

'I'm guessing that's you, Bella,' I say. 'Unless your father's feet have shrunk and he's borrowed your shoes.'

Bella slides out from under the car with a torch in her hand. She pulls a bandana off her head and lets her curly black hair fall down her back.

'Hi, Chloe,' she says. 'I think Dad needs new brake pads. We're waiting for a mechanic to see if I'm right.'

Any other parent would freak out at the

thought of their ten-year-old kid fiddling with their vehicle, especially a fancy convertible, but Bella designed and built the Anti-Princess Club headquarters, AKA an amazing treehouse with its own top-floor planetarium. I call her a builder-slash-artist.

'Should we head out the back to HQ?' she asks. 'You can help me set up for the meeting.'

We four original anti-princesses meet three times per month at Bella's treehouse and every fourth week at my apartment so the girls can hang out with my grandmother. Everyone loves Yiayia.

We were actually due for a meeting at my place next week, but instead we're all heading to my holiday house with my family. It will be the anti-princesses' first ever school-holiday getaway together. We have sleepovers all the time, but this will be for eight whole nights.

Emily and Grace aren't here yet, so I follow Bella through her mansion. It's seriously huge. Perky pop music with a man singing in Hindi is blaring from the downstairs lounge room. Bella's brother, Max, and their dad are watching a Bollywood film – the bright colours and choreographed dancing on the screen make it unmistakable. Bella's mum was born in India and introduced them to Bollywood, which is the nickname of the Indian film industry.

'Hi, Max,' I say. 'Hello, Dr MacKenzie.'

Bella's dad has a different surname to the rest of the family. Max and Bella use their mum's name, Singh.

'Don't be offended that they're not answering,'

Bella says. 'You'll never get their attention while they're watching those movies.'

'Are your parents worried about you coming away with my family for a whole week?' I ask. 'I bet they'll miss you.'

Bella grabs four bottles of orange juice from her fridge to take to the treehouse. 'They've got crazy rosters at the hospital next week, so I doubt that,' she says. 'Max will probably be a bit bored without me though.'

We walk through Bella's backyard and climb up into the treehouse. I take a drink from Bella as Grace's head pops through the doorway. 'Want a bottle, Grace?' Bella asks.

Grace lowers herself into a hip flexor stretch. 'As long as it's not blue,' she says. 'My earlobe has only just healed.'

Emily appears next and flips open her laptop before she even says hello. She uses her computer to communicate with the other 872 members of the Anti-Princess Club. We couldn't fit them all into the treehouse, or even Bella's mansion, so Emily built a website for everyone to meet virtually.

Emily is also our club president, so we can never start a meeting without her.

'I call this meeting of the Anti-Princess Club to order,' she says. 'Does anyone have any urgent matters of business?'

No one raises their hand.

Emily closes her laptop and rubs her palms together excitedly. 'I guess that means we can chat about next week's trip instead,' she says. 'I can't wait.'

We're interrupted by Dr MacKenzie calling up to us from underneath the treehouse. 'Bella!' he yells. 'The mechanic's here. Do you want to come and check out the engine together?'

Bella leaps up eagerly. 'Sorry, guys,' she says. 'I need to show this mechanic a thing or two.'

CHAPTER THREE

10 pairs of undies ✓
8 T-shirts ✓
4 pairs of shorts ✓
2 pairs of trackpants ✓
2 pairs of jeans ✓
1 hat ✓
1 swimsuit ✓

I think Emily likes packing. It's the mathematician in her. Numbers and order help her feel calm.

'Are you bringing your computer?' I ask.

She looks at me as if I've just asked whether she's taking her left leg. 'Of course. I can't cut off all the other anti-princesses just because they're not coming with us.'

Of all my best friends, Emily lives closest to me. My apartment and her house are both within walking distance from school, so we're at one or the other almost every day. That means I also spend a lot of time with Ava, Emily's little sister.

Ava throws a plastic bag onto Emily's bed. 'Mum wants you to pack these. It's sunscreen, cleanser, toner, moisturiser and a bunch of other stuff I can't remember the names of.'

Emily takes the sunscreen and ignores the rest. Her mum is a beautician, so she's always trying to get us into boring beauty regimes.

'I won't tell Mum you ditched all this if you take me with you,' Ava says. 'Pleeeeeease?'

'You know *I'm* lucky to be allowed to go away for so long, Ava,' Emily says. 'And I'm ten. There's no way Mum and Dad would've let me out of their sight for a week when I was six.'

Emily fires up her laptop. 'Let's look up Pacific

Palms,' she says. 'I want to see what it's like.'

Mum and Dad own a Greek restaurant downstairs from our apartment and they're run off their feet with work most of the time. But a couple of times a year, they like to escape to the most relaxing spot they know.

'It says here the entire population is only seven hundred,' Emily says. 'That's zero point one per cent of the population of Newcastle.'

I must admit, I've been a little worried that the other anti-princesses might be bored in The Palms. 'It sure is small,' I say. 'And a bit… slow.'

Emily senses my fear. 'Don't worry,' she says. 'We could entertain each other on a desert island if we had to.'

I hope she's right. Emily, Grace, Bella and I have never had a fight. I'd hate for us to get sick of each other at my sleepy old holiday house.

CHAPTER FOUR

Yiayia whacks Mum in the gut with her handbag.

'I can do it myself, *koritsi mou*,' she says. 'I'm not an invalid.'

Yiayia means 'grandmother' in Greek. *Koritsi mou* is what Yiayia calls my mum, and it means 'my girl'.

'Please let me help you,' Mum says. 'It's a high step.'

Emily, Grace, Bella and I are waiting in the back of the van for Yiayia and Mum. We're all heading to The Palms together. Dad is driving separately to pick up Alex from his boarding school on the way.

Yiayia hoists herself into the front passenger side.

'That's my Yiayia,' I say. 'Determined to look after herself, even at seventy-eight years young.'

Mum starts up the van and slowly reverses out of the driveway.

'What's wrong?' Yiayia asks. 'You're driving like a yiayia.'

The anti-princesses giggle as Mum sticks her head out the window. 'It's Grace's surfboard,' she says. 'I've never driven with anything strapped to the roof before.'

Bella climbs halfway out the window to take a squiz. 'It's fine, Mrs Karalis,' she says. 'The roof racks are solid and the straps are all pulled extremely tight.'

Mum looks at me for reassurance.

'Bella knows what she's talking about,' I say. 'She can even fix the van if it breaks down.'

The engine revs again and we're finally away.

'Woo hoo!' I shout. 'Off to The Palms we go!'

Emily pulls a computer game from her bag.

Yiayia turns around and tut-tuts. 'Put that away for the drive, *paidi mou*,' she says. 'Let's enjoy each other's company.'

Emily blushes and slips the game away. Yiayia doesn't understand that she can multi-task when it comes to computers, but Emily's not about to argue. 'So tell us what Pacific Palms is like, Yiayia,' she says. 'How does it compare to the beach towns in Greece?'

Yiayia loves reminiscing about her homeland. 'Nothing compares to the Greek Islands,' she says. 'My family always holidayed on an island called Hydra when I was a little girl. The beaches there are pebbled, not sandy. We would just swim off the rocks into the deep, green water.

'The streets on Hydra are made from cobbled stone and the only means of transport is donkeys. To this day, they don't allow cars or scooters on the island. It's too beautiful.'

Mum doesn't remember Greece. She was just a baby when Yiayia brought her over here.

Dad also came to Australia from Greece with his family. It's kind of funny that my parents didn't meet in the country where they were both born. They met when they were studying at chef school. That's when they decided to get married and start the restaurant.

'Why did you leave Greece, Yiayia?' Bella asks. 'I don't think you've ever told me.'

Yiayia sighs. 'There was a war,' she says. 'Things were never the same after that. No jobs. No money. The government spent the next two decades encouraging people to move abroad, so that's what we did.'

I press my cheek against the glass and watch the houses whoosh by in a blur. 'I'm glad you came here,' I say. 'I love the beaches. I love our apartment. I love my school.'

Grace nudges me in the ribs. I deliberately left my friends out to be cheeky.

'And, of course, I love my friends,' I say. 'I wouldn't have met the anti-princesses if you'd stayed in Greece.'

I meet Mum's gaze in the rear-view mirror. I can tell by the creases around her eyes that she's smiling. 'I'm glad to hear that, Chloe,' she says. 'All we want is for our children to be happy.'

I reach forward and pat Yiayia's shoulder. 'Of course I'm happy. I'm going on holiday with my mum, dad, brother, best friends and my precious yiayia. I couldn't be happier.'

CHAPTER FIVE

I wake with a jerk as Mum changes the van's gears.

I rub my eyes and look up. There's the sign by the side of the road: 'Welcome to Pacific Palms'.

Grace, Bella and Emily are all zonked out.

'Wake up, guys,' I say. 'We're here.'

Grace jolts awake first. She gasps as she spots the beach through the window. 'The waves look epic,' she says. 'I might get barrelled if it stays like this.'

Yiayia scratches her head and turns around with a look of confusion. 'What is "barrelled"?'

I happen to know about this, because there's a lot of physics involved. 'When waves travel from deep water to shallow water very quickly a barrel-like shape is created in the hollow section of the breaking wave.'

Grace takes over. 'So, getting barrelled means surfing in that tube of the wave. The surfer disappears behind a wall of sea and then comes out the opening as the wave curls over.'

'That would be awesome to see, Grace,' I say. 'Maybe we can catch it on camera to show your brothers.'

Grace has three brothers. She says she's glad to be getting away from them, but I think that by the end of the week she'll be wishing they were here.

'And here's our home away from home!' Mum announces.

It's nothing special from the street. Just a brick house surrounded by a little wooden deck. The best part is the location – the back-yard looks over the beach.

'Yay!' shouts Bella. 'What an amazing spot!'

Mum slides the van door open and we all pile out. I open Yiayia's side and help her down onto the grass. She's a bit stiff after such a long trip, so she's willing to push aside her pride and take my hand.

'That deck is calling my name,' she says. 'I plan to spend many hours sitting there with my tea, keeping an eye on you girls.'

As we turn towards the house, a girl's voice calls out from the road. 'Whose fish?'

There are two girls who look about thirteen and two boys about our age with boards under their arms.

'It's mine,' Grace tells them, laying her surfboard on the grass next to the van. 'It's a proper retro one.'

One of the girls starts laughing and the other kids copy her. 'You think you can ride a fish?' she asks. 'You might want to try your luck on a foamie out here, little girl.'

The group laughs again and jogs off.

'What were they talking about?' Emily asks. 'What's a foamie?'

'A board made from foam.' Grace grimaces as she slaps a bug on her neck, but I think she's more irritated by the surfer kids. 'It's what beginners start out on. My fish is foam covered in fibreglass – it's the next step up.'

'Don't listen to them, Grace,' I say. 'I've seen you ride this thing.'

'Who cares what they think?' Mum says, looking up from unloading the suitcases. 'They're just bored locals looking for trouble. You've got nothing to prove to them.'

Grace picks up her board. 'You're right, Mrs Karalis. That "little girl" stuff just irks me because I doubt they'd say that to one of my brothers.'

I feel angry for Grace. It's outrageous that some strangers think it's okay to pick on someone without knowing anything about them.

In all the years I've been coming to The

Palms I've never had a run-in with any of the kids who live here. Come to think of it, we've never really spoken. When they're not surfing, they tend to just hang around the slushy machine at the general store.

Maybe Mum's wrong. Maybe we *do* have something to prove to them if we want them to eat their words.

Those kids will be shocked once they see Grace on the water. She rips – and not just for a 'little girl'.

CHAPTER SIX

Boom. Shhhhhhhhhh.
Boom. Shhhhhhhhhh.

'Get up!' Bella shouts.
'I think we're in the middle of an earthquake!'

Emily and Grace spring awake, but I yawn and stretch my arms before I fully sit up.

I've done a lot of research into earthquakes. Geology is my favourite type of science. Or maybe it's biology, or ecology, or meteorology. Okay, so I like all types of science. 'That wasn't an earthquake,' I say. 'Earthquakes happen when the stress between two plates within the earth causes one or both plates to slip.'

Bella rolls her eyes. 'I know what an earth-quake is, Chloe. Didn't you hear that noise?'

Boom. Shhhhhhhhhh.

'There it is!' Bella yells.

Grace and I giggle. 'When the plates slip during an earthquake the surrounding land shakes,' I say. 'Have you felt any movement, Bella?'

Grace opens the bedroom curtains. 'That was what woke you up: those enormous, crashing waves.'

Emily rubs her eyes. 'You guys might not have felt any movement, but I did. There's a whole lot of rumbling going on in my tummy.'

Bella throws a pillow at Emily. 'Okay, okay,' she says. 'I'm sorry I'm not used to sleeping next to the ocean. Let's have breakfast and stop the earthquake in Emily's belly.'

Mum and Yiayia have stacks of pancakes waiting for us in the kitchen. The secret ingredient that makes them so thick and tasty is Greek yogurt. I came up with the recipe.

'Don't eat them all,' Yiayia says. 'We need to save some for your baba and Alex.'

As if on cue, Dad and Alex walk through the door. 'We went to the shops for supplies,' Alex says, piling some pancakes onto a plate and sprinkling blueberries on top.

'I bought this too,' Dad says, throwing a newspaper on the table. 'We can see if anything exciting is happening in town while we're here.'

Bella opens the paper and her eyes light up. *Billycart enthusiasts from across the region will gather in Pacific Palms this Saturday for the town's first ever billycart derby.*

'I'd watch that,' Grace says.

Bella jumps out of her chair. 'You guys can watch it,' she says. 'But I'm going in it.'

Dad coughs into his teacup. 'Er, nice idea, Bella,' he says. 'But we don't have a billycart.'

Dad doesn't know Bella as well as I thought he did. If we already had a billycart, she wouldn't be interested in racing.

'Leave it to me, Mr Karalis,' she says. 'I've always wanted to build one.'

Alex throws a blueberry into the air and catches it in his mouth. 'Impossible,' he says. 'You can't build a billycart in five days.'

I fold my arms. Bella, Emily and Grace do the same.

'Mission time,' Yiayia says. 'You should know better than to take on these girls, *Alexaki mou*.'

Emily bangs a fork against a glass. 'Would you like to propose a mission, Bella?'

'Yes,' Bella says, standing to attention. 'I will not only build a billycart by Saturday, I will race it in the Pacific Palms derby.'

Yiayia passes Emily a pen and she scribbles on the front page of the newspaper.

Mission Revhead: Build a billycart and race it in Saturday's derby.

'All in favour?' Emily asks.

Everyone raises their hands. Even Yiayia, Mum, Dad and Alex.

CHAPTER SEVEN

Emily and I are swinging in the hammock on the deck while Grace goes for a jog and Bella sketches some billycart designs inside.

'I don't know why people sleep in flat beds,' I say. 'A couple of Swiss scientists did some research a few years ago that proved swaying motions can help slow our brain activity into a sleeping pattern.'

Emily starts whispering numbers.

'What are you counting now?' I ask.

'Clouds,' she replies.

I look up at the sky. 'Those are cumulus clouds,' I say. 'White and puffy, like cotton wool.'

Emily points at one of the fatter clouds. 'I wonder how many droplets of water it took to make that one.'

I love conversations like this, when my love of science and Emily's passion for maths come together.

'Clouds can contain millions of tonnes of water,' I say. 'If you could figure out how many droplets are in a tonne, that would be a good place to start.'

Yiayia appears with the newspaper from breakfast. She tosses it into my lap. 'Read me some articles,' she says. 'I can't find my glasses.'

I open the paper. 'Hey, there's a fair coming to town – ah, the billycart derby is part of it. It says it's running for five whole days because of all the visitors passing through.'

Emily reads the story out loud for Yiayia. *'Hundreds of people are expected to visit Pacific Palms from Wednesday to Sunday for the eighty-fifth annual fair. Highlights include the quilt show, cake display, pumpkin-growing contest, pig races and the popular sideshow alley.'*

Yiayia licks her lips. 'Cake display? I would like to see that.'

I don't think I've ever been to The Palms' fair before. Our trips mustn't have coincided with the last eighty-four of them. 'Pig races sound funny,' I say. 'But what's a sideshow alley?'

Emily grunts disapprovingly. 'It's where you find games like the ring toss and lucky dips. They're all rigged.'

Yiayia pushes the hammock so it swings a

little faster. 'So cynical for such a young girl, Emily,' she says. 'You should go to the fair and have some fun.'

Emily looks up at the sky and I can tell she's already counting clouds again. 'I'll go,' she says. 'But if any of those swindlers try to trick me, they better watch out.'

CHAPTER EIGHT

The shuttlecock hits Yiayia on the nose and she falls backwards in shock.

I'm on her team, so I'm the first to reach her as Bella and Grace duck under the badminton net to join us. 'Are you okay?' I ask. 'Where does it hurt?'

Yiayia's a little dazed and doesn't answer.

'Show me your face, Yiayia,' I say. I know shuttlecocks aren't exactly dangerous missiles, but Yiayia bruises easily. Her skin seems to be becoming thinner and more sensitive as she gets older. 'I can't see any damage. Let's check the rest of you.'

Yiayia dusts off her knees. 'I'm fine, *paidi mou*,' she says. 'Help me up.'

Grace grips Yiayia's wrists and heaves her to her feet. 'I'm so sorry, Yiayia,' she says. 'It was me who hit the shuttlecock.'

Yiayia shakes our hands off. 'Back to the game.'

Yiayia sometimes confuses ambition with ability. She doesn't like to admit that she's getting a little frail.

'Let's take a little break,' I say. 'I could use some tea. Then we could go for a walk to the lake before the sun goes down.'

She knows I'm tricking her out of another round, but she can't resist the temptation of chamomile tea and the lake.

Every year, Yiayia and I walk to the lake and feed the seagulls. It's one of our special places. It's right near the ocean, and when the tide is up you can't reach it by foot because a river floods the track. We discovered it by accident when I was just a toddler.

'You're a clever girl, Chloe,' she says. 'I'll put the kettle on.'

Mum and Dad are already in the kitchen cooking lamb stew. 'Ah, just the person we need,' Dad says. 'Chloe, something is missing from this kleftiko – what do you think it is?'

I dip a spoon into the pot to taste the mixture. 'A lot more garlic,' I say. 'And some rosemary.'

Mum clicks her fingers. 'Of course, rosemary,' she says. 'What would we do without our little cook?'

I roll my eyes. My parents should know better than to call me a cook. Ever since I was little they've talked about Alex and me taking over the restaurant one day. I've made it clear I'm not interested. I'm going to be a Nobel Prize-winning scientist, not a restaurateur.

I think I have a flair for creating recipes because it's a bit like conducting scientific experiments: a pinch of this, a drop of that. But I'd much rather be mixing ingredients in test tubes in a laboratory.

'Ouch!' Yiayia yells. 'Cold water, cold water!'

Mum runs the cold tap. Yiayia sticks her hand under the stream.

'What happened?' I ask.

Yiayia curses under her breath in Greek.

'She has a little burn from the kettle,' Mum says. 'She'll be okay. The lake will have to wait, though.'

I signal for Bella and Emily to leave the kitchen with me. It hurts Yiayia's pride when this sort of thing happens in front of my friends.

'Poor Yiayia,' Emily says. 'She's having a bad day.'

I hope that's all it is. A single day.

CHAPTER NINE

Grace is surfing like a pro. Every time she turns the board a huge fan of spray shoots off the back.

'Go Grace!' I call from the sand. 'You're ripping!'

Even Emily looks up from her laptop to watch Grace's moves. 'She's getting really good,' she says. 'Her board was completely vertical for a second there.'

Bella nods towards the dunes. The local kids who hassled Grace when we arrived at The Palms are here. They all look over and smirk.

'Do you reckon they're related?' Bella asks. 'They look alike.'

All four kids are sandy blond with dark tans. The only differences are one girl and one boy have curls and the others have straight hair.

I shrug. 'Only one way to find out.' I stick two fingers between my lips. *Phweeeeeeeeeet.*

'Come over here if you want something,' curly-haired girl calls out.

Bella, Emily and I hop along the hot sand to the gang. 'Hi, I'm Chloe,' I say. 'This is Bella and Emily, and that's our friend Grace out surfing.'

Straight-haired girl laughs. It's not a real laugh. It's fake and rude. 'She's a kook. That's what us real surfers call people who are hopeless.'

Curly-haired girl high-fives straight-haired girl as if she's just told the joke of the century.

'I'm Kailani,' curly-haired girl says. 'This is my best friend Taylor and her brother Ash. And this is my brother Tex.'

All four of them stare at us, but none crack a smile.

'Well, nice to meet you,' I say. 'We'll be over here watching you guys catch a few waves.'

Kailani, Taylor, Ash and Tex run to the water while Bella, Emily and I sit back down.

'What jerks,' Bella says. 'Let's not talk to them again.'

Emily gazes at the water while she waits for her laptop to fire up. 'Hey, what's that Tex doing?'

Tex and Ash are paddling their boards to the inside of Grace so she won't be able to take off on the next wave.

'Maybe Grace is letting them go first,' I say. 'That's the sort of thing she'd do.'

A wave rolls in and Ash catches it. Another comes not far behind and Tex takes it.

'This one's Grace's,' Bella says as the next wave comes along.

Grace turns to catch the wave when Kailani appears on her inside and starts paddling.

'Hey, that's dangerous!' I yell.

Kailani stands up and surfs all the way to shore. She sticks her tongue out at us as she runs along the sand.

'How mature,' I say. 'I hope I can come up with something smarter than pulling faces when I'm a teenager.'

Grace starts to paddle onto another wave but Taylor pushes in front of her.

'It's called dropping in,' Bella says. 'It means taking another surfer's wave at the last minute, or blocking them from having a decent ride.'

I can't see Grace's face, but she slams her hands down in the water to make a big splash. She's cranky.

'Let's go, Grace!' I call out. 'Time for lunch!'

As Grace floats back to us on a small wave, Ash, Tex, Kailani and Taylor start taunting her.

'Better luck next time!' Taylor calls.

'They run surf lessons for tourists, you know!' Tex jeers.

Grace undoes her ankle strap and drops her

board on the sand. 'What is *with* those guys?'

I wrap a towel around her shoulders. 'I don't think they're used to strangers,' I say. 'Especially awesome surfing strangers like you.'

CHAPTER TEN

Bella thumps on the garage door for the third time.

'All right, I hear ya!' a voice calls from inside. 'Hold your horses!'

Bella taps her foot impatiently. 'The sign says *Jim's Motor Repairs – Open Monday to Friday*,' she says. 'So why is the door closed?'

A grey-haired man in grease-smeared overalls rolls the door up. His name tag says *Jim*. He seems amused to find four ten-year-old girls on the other side. 'Can I help you?'

Bella gets straight down to business. 'Hello, sir,' she says. 'I'm not from here—'

The man cuts her off. 'You don't say. I've never had a little girl knock on my door before. They don't tend to drive cars, you see.'

Bella politely smiles at Jim's lame attempt to be funny. 'Well, I'm after some parts,' she says. 'I'm building a billycart for the derby.'

Jim laughs so hard he loses his breath. 'Hang on a tic, I've got to share this.' He cups his hands around his mouth and yells, 'Ralphy! Come over here, will ya?'

A younger man in the same sort of overalls emerges from a shop across the road.

'Ralph's Mechanics,' Bella says. 'That's the only other mechanic in town. It was going to be my next stop.'

Ralph drops a cigarette butt on the ground and crosses the road. I've already decided I don't like him – not only is he significantly cutting his life expectancy by smoking, he's littering with something that takes at least five years to break down.

'What do we have here, then?' he asks. 'You

girls looking for some cleaning work? I could use someone to sweep my floor.'

I groan while Grace clenches her fists and Emily folds her arms.

Bella keeps her composure as she tries to strike some sort of deal. 'I guess I'd be willing to sweep your floor in exchange for some materials, sir,' she says. 'I need everything from wheels to timber. Whatever you can spare.'

Ralph scratches his head while Jim laughs some more. 'This here girl wants to build a billycart,' Jim explains. 'She's not from around these parts.'

Ralph chortles, pulls a fresh cigarette from his pocket and turns back to his shop. 'I don't have time for this malarky,' he says. 'I've got six oil changes to get done this afternoon.'

Bella's confused. We all are.

'Why won't you help us?' I ask.

Jim starts to roll down his garage door. 'Do you know what day it is?'

'Tuesday,' we all answer.

'The race is Saturday,' Jim says. 'The kids around here have been building their carts for months. You girls aren't gonna build a billycart in four days.'

Before we can argue he closes the door all the way. We hear a click on the other side.

'He's locked it,' Bella says. 'I can't believe it.'

We're all in a bit of shock. Jim and Ralph were downright rude.

'He doesn't know you, Bella,' I say. 'If he did, he'd know you can build a billycart by Saturday.'

Yap, yap, yap. Yap. Yap.
A tiny dog is barking
at us from behind a
gate next to Ralph's
Mechanics.

'Oh, how cute,'
Emily says. 'Let's give
him a pat.'

We run across the road and hang our hands over the gate.

'Watch out!' a voice calls. 'He bites!'

Everyone jumps back. There's so much junk in the yard it's hard to see where the voice came from.

'There,' Bella says. 'Near the front door.'

An elderly lady, even older than Yiayia, is sitting in a rocking chair. 'You girls need a mechanic?'

Bella's eyes are darting all over the yard.

'No,' I say. 'My friend was just looking for some bits and pieces to build a billycart.'

The lady reaches for a walking stick and hobbles to the front of her porch. 'Well, come on in,' she says. 'Help yourself.'

Bella jumps for joy. 'Are you sure?' she asks. 'You've got so much great stuff here.'

The lady waves her walking stick around. 'It's rubbish. You'll be doing me a favour.'

Before anyone can blink, Bella is loading up a rusty trolley with old fence palings.

'Is that a bike under those vines?' Grace asks.

The lady puts her glasses on. 'Ah, yes,' she says. 'Haven't ridden that in about twenty years. If you can untangle it, take it.'

I spy an old plastic chair under a shrub. 'Bella, could you use this?'

She claps excitedly. 'Yes! It could be the driver's seat!'

'What else do you need, Bella?' Emily asks. 'A steering wheel of some sort?'

Bella scans the yard. 'No need for a steering wheel,' she says. 'That rope will do nicely.'

The lady looks like she's about to doze off in her rocking chair.

'What's your name?' Bella asks her.

She opens one eye. 'Joan. Like Joan of Arc.'

Bella jumps onto the porch and shakes Joan's hand. 'Well, you've certainly saved my day,' she says. 'You're a saint, just like the real Joan of Arc.'

CHAPTER ELEVEN

Emily is buying a bag of fairy floss at least three times the size of her head.

'That will be two dollars, please,' the stallholder says.

'How much money do you have left, Emily?' I ask.

'Eight dollars,' she says. 'Enough for four more bags of fairy floss – my favourite food. The fair only runs for another four days, so we could come back for another bag each day.'

Grace points at a wall of balloons. There's a boy throwing darts at them. 'You should use some of your money for that, Emily. You've got an eye for angles and precision. Plus, five straight days of fairy floss might turn you off your favourite food for life.'

'The carnies rig those games,' Emily says. 'I won't be wasting my money on them.'

'What are carnies?' I ask.

'People who travel from town to town following the fair circuit,' Emily says. 'They never stay in one place long enough to get caught for rigging the games.'

The boy's final dart bounces off a balloon and falls to the ground. We edge closer and watch another boy hand over two dollars.

The carnie passes him three darts. 'Take your time,' she says. 'If you pop a balloon, you win a teddy bear.'

The first dart misses the balloons altogether. The second hits a balloon but it doesn't bust. 'Drats,' the boy says. 'I'll throw the next one harder.' He pulls his arm back, as though he's pitching a softball, and throws the dart with all his might.

It hits a balloon right in the middle of the wall, but again it doesn't budge.

The boy stomps his foot in frustration and calls out to his mum, 'I need more money!'

'Why didn't the balloons burst?' I whisper in Emily's ear.

Emily pulls two dollars from her pocket. 'Okay, here goes,' she says. 'Let me show you the problem.'

The stallholder gives her the same three darts the boy used.

Emily holds the first dart up to her eye and shakes her head. 'This won't work. The tip of the dart has been broken off.'

The carnie snatches the dart from Emily. 'Here's another.'

Emily takes the second dart and runs her finger over the tip. 'This won't work either. It's been filed down. Darts are supposed to be sharp.'

A few more kids and parents are gathering around. The carnie is getting flustered. 'Pipe down, will you,' she says out of the corner of her mouth. 'Try this one.'

Emily inspects the third dart, then looks up. 'This dart is pointy enough,' she says. 'But there's also a problem with the balloons.'

'Okay folks, I'm calling it a day here!' the carnie shouts to the growing crowd. 'Be sure to come back tomorrow!'

She grabs the third dart from Emily's hand and gives her back her two dollars. 'Buzz off,' she hisses. 'You've made your point.'

A boy speaks up. 'What's wrong with the balloons?'

'They're not blown up properly,' Emily says. 'Under-inflated balloons will deflect most darts even if you throw them well. The chances of winning a prize here are very low.'

'We want our money back!' yells the boy who tried his luck before Emily.

We quietly step away as the crowd erupts.

'Wow,' I say. 'I wonder how many of the games here are dodgy.'

Emily hands me her fairy floss and takes a notepad from her pocket. 'You've just inspired my mission for the trip,' she says. 'What do you think of this?'

Mission Carnie Cracker:
Expose the fair's tricksters.

Something about Emily's mission makes me feel a little uneasy. 'Do you think they deserve it?' I ask. 'I mean, they're not really hurting anyone.'

Emily's bottom lip drops. 'I thought you'd support me as a scientist, Chloe. The beautiful thing about maths and science is that they rely on accuracy and truth – not lies and hocus pocus like these carnie games.'

I nod. I guess the carnie folk could still do their jobs honestly.

'All in favour?' Emily asks.

Grace, Bella and I raise our hands.

'Good,' Emily says. 'By the time this holiday is over, the Pacific Palms *Un*fair will be the fairest of them all.'

CHAPTER TWELVE

I smile as I feel Yiayia's fingertip on my forehead.

She likes to wake me up by tracing heart shapes around my face. 'Rise and shine, *paidi mou*,' she whispers. 'Twenty minutes until sunrise.'

I stretch my arms above my head. 'I'll wake the others.'

I enjoy sleeping in sometimes, but there's nothing like watching the sun rise over the ocean. When I was younger, Yiayia used to take me to the beach every morning on our holidays. This year I promised the anti-princesses we would all head down to the sand at least once before the sun came out.

'I'm up,' Grace whispers from across the room. 'I'm used to early starts for athletics practice.'

Emily wakes with a startled snort. 'Is it time already?'

I roll over to Bella and lift her eye mask. She needs to block out every speck of light to sleep properly. 'Morning, Bella,' I say. 'Time to go to the beach.'

Bella pulls a pillow over her face and asks in a muffled voice, 'Should we wear our swimsuits?'

Grace leaps out of bed and pulls on her boardshorts. 'Great idea, Bella,' she says. 'An ocean dip first thing in the morning is excellent for getting the blood pumping.'

I grab a beach towel and tiptoe into the kitchen. There's a basket on the table.

'Look inside,' Yiayia says quietly.

I open the lid and start drooling. There's a fruit salad, a huge tub of yoghurt, five cinnamon doughnuts and a thermos of chamomile tea.

'A breakfast picnic,' I whisper. 'What an awesome idea, Yiayia.'

'We can go the lake after the sun comes up,' Yiayia says. 'The seagulls must be wondering why we haven't visited yet.'

I pass the basket to Grace and take a couple of torches from the cupboard. We follow Emily out the back door.

Every bird in town seems to be singing the dawn chorus.

'Listen to that,' I say. 'It's mostly male birds singing loudly to show off to potential mates. It's like they're telling all the female birds that they've woken up strong and healthy.'

I take Yiayia by the forearm to help her down the stairs. 'Watch your step, Yiayia. It's still pretty dark.'

She clutches the handrail. 'I may not be a male bird, but I have woken up strong and healthy, *paidi mou.*'

I let her walk on her own, but by the time

we reach the hard sand near the water's edge I notice she has broken out in a sweat. I lay out my towel and help her sit down.

'Don't worry, Yiayia,' Grace says. 'Walking across soft sand is a workout for all of us.'

I wink at Grace to thank her for trying to make Yiayia feel less self-conscious.

We sit in silence as a glint of pink appears on the horizon. Shades of red, purple and orange slowly swallow the black until the sun peeks over the edge of the ocean and floats into the sky.

'Beautiful,' Bella says. 'I wish I had some paints and a canvas here to capture it.'

The sky turns to blue and I can't resist

another scientific fact. 'You know, the sun *appears* to rise above the horizon and circle the Earth,' I say. 'But it's actually the Earth that's rotating while the sun stays still.'

'Well, I can't stay still any longer.' Grace kicks off her thongs. 'Last one in the water is a rotten egg!'

Bella and Emily take off after her.

'Do you want me to sit with you, Yiayia?' I ask. 'I don't mind.'

Yiayia shoos me away. 'Don't be silly. Go!'

I run into the water at full speed. I'm feeling brave, so I swim out a little further than the others. I duck dive, and as my head breaks through the surface of the water I look back.

Grace, Bella and Emily are madly swimming to the shore.

I squint beyond them at the sand and see Yiayia.

She's lying in a heap.

I kick frantically and bodysurf the next wave in, crash-land next to Grace and push her out of the way. Yiayia's eyes are open but she doesn't seem to see me. I gently tap her cheek and she blinks three times.

'I think I need a doughnut,' she says.

Grace hugs me quickly. 'I'm going to head back to the house and get your parents.'

Yiayia frowns as Grace takes off. 'It's nothing,' she says. 'It happens when you get to my age.'

It's my turn to frown. 'Enough, Yiayia. Fainting *is* a big deal.'

Emily and Bella look at each other awkwardly. They've never heard me be so stern with Yiayia.

'How about I fetch the tea from the picnic basket?' Emily asks. 'Come on, Bella, you can help.'

I rest my chin on top of Yiayia's head and wrap my arms around her shoulders. 'You scared me,' I say. 'Don't do it again, you hear?'

CHAPTER THIRTEEN

Yiayia's fast asleep with Mum by her bedside.

'I've made a doctor's appointment for her,' Mum whispers to me. 'She probably just overdid it. Sometimes she can walk for miles, but other days she just doesn't have the energy.'

I hang my head. I feel responsible for Yiayia's fainting.

'It's not your fault,' Mum says. 'Go back to the beach with the girls. The lake will have to wait again.'

I kiss Mum and Yiayia and head outside. Grace is waxing her surfboard while Emily rubs sunscreen on Bella's back.

'Is Yiayia all right?' Grace asks.

I nod. 'Let's go to the beach.'

Grace groans when we reach the sand. Kailani, Taylor, Ash and Tex are already in the water. 'They're in the best position,' Grace says. 'I won't catch anything now.'

A couple of men, about the same age as our dads, are paddling out to the same spot.

'You'll be okay, Grace,' Emily says. 'Those adults will pull the kids into line if they give you any trouble.'

Grace bends over and touches her toes. 'You're right. At least it won't be four against one like it was the other day.'

Bella, Emily and I follow Grace into the water to swim in the shallows as she paddles out to where the waves are breaking.

One of the men launches onto a wave and does an impressive turn before flicking off.

'He's a great surfer,' Bella says. 'Doesn't look like he'll be taking any nonsense from the jerks out there.'

Tex gets into position to catch the next wave. Just as he is about to jump to his feet, the other man drops in on him.

'Ooh, that was close,' I say. 'They nearly collided.'

Tex sticks his middle finger up at the man and makes way for Ash to take off. The other man drops in on him too.

Then it happens to Kailani, and again to Taylor.

Kailani, Taylor, Ash and Tex are yelling and making rude hand gestures at the men.

'Looks like those older guys are even bigger jerks than the local kids,' Bella says. 'They won't let anyone get a wave.'

Grace paddles into the line-up and gets ready to try her luck. But, sure enough, one of the men cuts her off.

The swell dies down for a moment and the seven surfers are all bobbing next to one another. Kailani thumps the nose of her board and screams at the men, 'The next one's mine!'

One of the men splashes water into her face. 'No one owns the ocean, kid,' he says. 'It's not our problem if you're too slow to take off before us.'

Ash grabs a clump of seaweed floating by his board and hurls it at him, only just missing. 'Go back to where you came from! This is our beach!'

The men put their heads down and start paddling towards him.

Grace does the same and lines up her board to act as a barrier between the kids and the adults. 'Cool it!' she yells. 'Someone could get hurt out here.'

The men are fuming. One has his chest puffed out and fists clenched and the other has veins pulsating in his forehead and neck.

Grace turns to Kailani and Taylor. 'Let's head in,' she says. 'The waves aren't that great anyway.'

Surprisingly, the girls listen to Grace and paddle back to us with their brothers in tow.

'That's the way!' The men start laughing. 'Back home to your mummies and daddies, grommets!'

Grace and the other kids reach the sand and pull off their leg ropes. They dump their boards and sit staring out to sea.

Bella, Emily and I join them. I'm not sure who should speak first. We're still not exactly friends with Kailani, Taylor, Ash and Tex.

Taylor breaks the silence by bursting into tears.

'There'll be more waves later,' Grace tells her. 'It's not the end of the world.'

'You don't get it.' Ash pegs a shell into the water. 'You're stupid tourists just like them.'

I stand up and put my hands on my hips. 'Now listen here. If it wasn't for Grace, you may have got your head punched in by one of those guys.'

Kailani stands up and meets me eye-to-eye. 'Every holidays, you tourists swarm into town and take all our waves.'

I step back from her. Kailani's worked up and a little too close for my comfort. 'You need to get your facts straight,' I say. 'Grace is the only one of us who even surfs.'

Taylor is next to rise. 'Well, your friend can't just turn up and take our waves. That's not how it works.'

Grace jumps up with Bella and Emily behind her. 'I don't want to take anyone's waves,' Grace says. 'There are plenty for everyone if we just follow the rules.'

'You really don't know what you're on about,' Tex scoffs. 'There are no *rules* in surfing, stupid.'

Grace pauses for a moment to think. 'You're actually right, Tex,' she says. 'I always thought that taking turns on waves was a rule…but it's not. It's just good manners.'

Kailani, Taylor and Ash look shocked, like they didn't expect Grace to be so considerate, especially after Tex called her stupid.

'Do you play any other sports?' Grace asks.

Tex nods. 'I play soccer.'

'I play soccer too,' Grace says. 'And you know what makes it work? Rules. Otherwise it would be a big mess of people running around a field like chooks with no heads.'

I'm not sure where Grace is going with this, but the jerky foursome is softening up. Tex and Ash shuffle closer to her, and Kailani and Taylor are actually smiling at her.

'I'd like to propose a mission,' Grace says. 'I think we should come up with a surfers' code of conduct. We can put a sign up on the paths to the beach with a list of rules for everyone to follow – locals *and* tourists.'

Emily grabs a stick and writes into the sand.

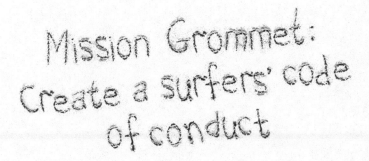

Mission Grommet:
Create a surfers' code
of conduct

'All in favour?' Emily asks.

Grace, Bella and I raise our hands.

Kailani, Taylor, Ash and Tex look truly baffled, but they stick their arms in the air too.

'Can one of the rules be *no tourists allowed*?' Tex asks.

Grace ruffles his hair like she does to her own brothers. 'Very funny,' she says. 'And no.'

CHAPTER FOURTEEN

Tap, tap, tap. Tap, tap, tap.

Bella started working on her billycart as soon as we got back from the beach. So far, she's detached the wheels from the bicycle and trolley we salvaged from Joan of Arc's yard. Now, she's nailing the fence palings together.

'Thank goodness your parents had a toolkit in the house, Chloe,' she says. 'All I brought along was a wrench and a tape measure.'

I hold a paling steady as Bella hammers another nail into the wood. 'Do you think you'll be ready by Saturday?'

'Of course I will. The cart I'm making is

basic – with a couple of special additions.'
Bella picks up a brick in each hand and smiles
mischievously. 'I found these under the house.
They're my secret weapon.'

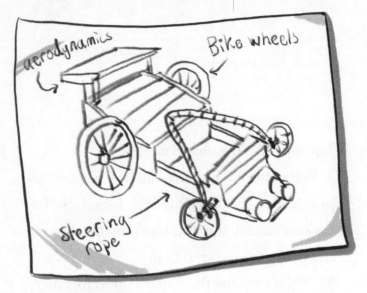

I take a brick to feel how heavy it is. 'Great
idea,' I say. 'From a physics perspective some
added weight should make you go faster,
especially if there aren't any corners and your
cart isn't very aerodynamic.'

Emily and Grace emerge from the house,
still in their swimsuits.

'Check out Bella's billycart,' I say. 'It'll be finished soon.'

Grace looks doubtful. 'No offence, but it still looks like a pile of junk.'

Emily elbows Grace in the ribs. 'I see what you're doing,' she says. 'The fence palings are the frame.'

We all huddle around and watch as Bella makes axles out of two metal rods from the trolley. She fixes two small trolley wheels at the front of the billycart frame and two bigger wheels from the bike at the back.

'Smart move,' Emily says. 'Bigger wheels at the back will cause an effect where the rear wheels try to catch the front ones. You'll go faster that way.'

Bella gives Emily the thumbs up. 'That was my plan. Now, guys, step away for this next part.' She pulls on some safety goggles. 'Mrs Karalis!' she yells. 'I need to use the drill now!'

Bella's parents don't have a problem with her using power tools. She actually taught her dad how to use an angle grinder. My parents are a little more cautious.

Mum comes out of the house carrying the drill as if it's a loaded weapon. 'Are you sure you know what you're doing, Bella?'

'Yes, Mrs Karalis.' Bella nods politely. 'It will be done in a few seconds.' She turns on the drill and attaches the plastic seat to the timber with four screws.

She hands the drill back to Mum. 'Danger over. Easy peasy.'

Grace picks up the rope. 'What's this for again?'

'I'll use it to steer,' Bella says. 'Kind of like reins on a horse.' She ties the rope to the front axle, takes a seat and pulls it from side to side to demonstrate.

Emily and Grace applaud, but I fear Bella has missed something.

'Um,' I say. 'What about brakes?'

Bella laughs. 'You know what billycarts are called in some parts of the world?' she asks. 'Gravity racers. And, as a scientist, you know all about gravity, right?'

Of course I know about gravity. It's the natural force that causes things to fall towards the earth. 'So billycarts rely on gravity to move?' I ask.

Bella pushes the billycart across the grass and it stops a few metres away. 'Yes, which means we won't be racing on flat ground like this,' she says. 'It will be downhill...down a very steep hill, probably.'

I gulp. Bella avoided properly answering the question about brakes, which I figure can only mean one thing: she doesn't actually have any.

CHAPTER FIFTEEN

Not even a pen full of squealing piglets can distract Emily from her mission.

Hundreds of people are gathering around the arena at the fairground to watch the main attraction, but Emily won't stop. 'Let's get to the sideshow alley,' she says. 'I've got tricks to crack.'

'Do you think we can be back here in half an hour?' I ask. 'I really want to watch the piglet racing.'

'We'll be back with time to spare,' Emily says, marching ahead.

She stops at a booth with ten white milk

bottles stacked in the shape of a pyramid.

A carnie in an oversized cowboy hat pounces on us. 'You girlies want to take a turn at knocking over these bottles? It's the easiest game here.'

Emily eyes him suspiciously as she hands him two dollars.

The carnie gives her a softball in return. 'Roll it towards the bottles,' he says. 'And when they're all knocked down you can pick a prize.'

Emily hands the ball to Grace. 'Does that feel strange to you?'

Grace rolls the ball between her hands then tosses it into the air. 'It's far too light.'

Emily hands the ball back to the carnie. 'I bet if I pulled the leather cover off this I'd find it filled with pure cork. A normal softball's core is made from a mix of cork and rubber – or a polyurethane mix.'

'Poly what?' he asks. Emily's words have gone way over his head.

I step in. 'Polyurethane. It's a synthetic resin mostly used to make different kinds of foam.'

The carnie seems to have no interest in my explanation, even though I tried my best to make it as unscientific as possible. 'So are you going to have a turn or not?'

Emily takes the ball and rolls it towards the bottles. One falls off the top of the pyramid, but the rest don't move.

'Take another shot,' the carnie says. 'You get three turns all up.'

Emily pauses and examines the bottles. 'What's in them?' she asks.

The carnie purses his lips. 'There's nothing in them,' he says. 'They're empty bottles.'

Emily steps inside the booth. 'Mind if I feel them?'

The carnie shakes his head furiously. 'You can't do that. No one is allowed inside the booth except me. It's for safety reasons.'

Emily ignores him and lifts a bottle from the top tier. 'That's empty.'

'Security!' the carnie yells. 'I need this girl removed from my booth!'

Emily takes a bottle from the next row. 'And that's empty too.'

The carnie rushes towards her, trying to slip his body between Emily and the bottles. He's too slow. Emily wraps both hands around a bottle on the bottom row, bends at the knees and heaves, but it's too heavy to lift. 'This certainly isn't empty.'

A couple of families stop to see what the commotion is. 'What's going on here?' a woman asks.

Emily unscrews the top of one of the milk bottles. 'It's sand,' she announces. 'Almost all the bottles on the bottom row of the pyramid are filled with sand. That's why no one can knock them all over – they're too heavy.'

The carnie's face turns bright red. I'm afraid he might erupt, so I call Emily away. 'I think it's time to move on.'

Before Emily can escape, the carnie flees

the scene, grabbing his moneybag and running through the crowd.

'Where's he going?' Bella asks.

We watch as he weaves through the families in the sideshow alley, disappearing behind a pavilion in the distance.

'I guess he didn't want to face the crowd once he was exposed,' Emily says. 'So he's just…gone.'

Three more carnies see us coming and immediately shut up shop. One pulls an awning down across the front of his booth, another sits a 'Closed' sign on his table, and the last shouts, 'I'm out – enjoy the rest of your day!'

Just two remain open at the end of the alley – a basketball game and a pond of plastic ducks.

'Ooh, basketball,' Grace says. 'I'm great at shooting hoops.'

'Okay, Grace.' Emily hands a dollar to the carnie in charge of the basketball game. 'Take a shot.'

Grace lifts the basketball and aims at the ring. It misses, then hits the ground and bounces high into the air.

'Hmmmm,' Emily says. 'That bounced higher than I would've expected. I think it's over-inflated.'

The carnie flashes her gold-capped teeth at Emily. 'I can see what you're trying to prove,' she says. 'But I've got nothing to hide here. Take another ball if you don't like that one.'

Emily grabs a ball and takes a shot herself. It looks as if the ball should go through the ring, but it hits it awkwardly and bounces off.

'Bad luck,' the carnie says. 'One shot left.'

Emily turns to Bella. 'I don't suppose you're carrying a measuring device, my trusty builder friend?'

Bella reaches into her pocket and pulls out a tape measure.

Emily turns back to the carnie. 'If I were to climb on my friend Grace's shoulders, would you let me measure that ring?'

The carnie puts her hands on her hips. 'No,' she says. 'I would not let you measure that ring.'

Emily twists the tape around her fingers. 'And why not?'

'Because the ring is undersized, okay?' the carnie whispers. 'It's a very tight squeeze to get the ball through.'

Emily's taken aback by the carnie's honesty. 'Ah, so you admit it?'

'I know your type.' The carnie starts dismantling the ring. 'You've proved your smarts, now be on your way.'

Emily backs away with the rest of us.

'That was weird,' I say. 'She didn't even try to hide the fact she was tricking people.'

We reach the pond of plastic ducks and Emily hands over two dollars.

'Ain't nothing shady going on here,' the carnie says. 'Simply fish a duck out of the pond and you'll win a prize.' He gestures to a shelf of numbered prizes and passes Emily a stick with a hook on the end.

We all study the hook carefully, but it seems intact. Emily easily hooks a plastic duck and brings it in. The carnie flips it over and reads a number from the bottom. 'Thirty-*nine!*'

He takes a whistle marked '39' from the shelf and passes it to Emily. 'Told you,' he says. 'Simple as that.'

A horn blares in the distance. 'It's the pig races!' I say. 'Let's go.'

The carnie waves us off. 'Come back tomorrow if you like,' he says. 'Everyone wins at the duck pond, ladies and gentlemen!'

As we run back to the arena, a voice booms over the loudspeaker. '*Mr Porky wins round one!*'

Emily stops in her tracks. 'Porkies,' she says. 'That carnie is telling porkies. I'll prove it.'

CHAPTER SIXTEEN

Cough, cough, cough. Cough. Cough.

I'm squished between a man with his arm in a sling and a girl coughing as though she's about to lose a lung.

Mum and Yiayia got the only other vacant seats on the opposite side of the waiting room.

Cough, cough, cough. Cough. Cough.

I get up. I'd rather stand than risk catching whatever has infected the coughing girl. The droplets in a single sneeze can contain millions of virus particles capable of surviving in the air for hours.

'I'm telling you, *koritsi mou*,' Yiayia says,

'I don't need to see a doctor.'

Mum pretends she doesn't hear and opens a magazine. 'Oh look, a recipe for lamb meatballs. They'd be good with the feta dipping sauce you invented, Chloe.'

A young woman in a T-shirt and cargo pants opens the surgery door. 'Eleni Petropoulos?'

Mum closes her magazine. 'We're here,' she says, and the doctor steps back inside her room to wait for us.

Yiayia is sceptical. 'That is no doctor,' she says. 'She's a child.'

I make a 'tsk-tsk' sound. It's what Yiayia does when she disapproves of something. 'Don't judge a book by its cover, Yiayia. She might be fresh out of university and a whole lot more enthusiastic than someone who's been in the job for fifty years.'

Mum and I walk Yiayia into the doctor's room. 'Welcome, Mrs Petropoulos,' the doctor says. 'What a beautiful Greek name you have.'

Yiayia takes a seat. 'You know Greek?'

The doctor smiles. 'No, but I've visited the Greek Islands,' she says. 'My name is Daria Weal. What can I do for you today?'

Mum interjects. If she didn't, Yiayia would spend the whole appointment reminiscing about the Greek Islands. 'My mother fainted on the beach yesterday,' she says. 'We're on holidays here for a week, from Newcastle.'

'Ah yes.' Dr Weal ruffles through some papers. 'The receptionist organised for your files to be sent to our practice.'

Yiayia is staring at a painting of a bowl of lemons on the wall.

'Mrs Petropoulos? Have you ever been tested for Type 2 diabetes?' Dr Weal asks.

Yiayia yawns.

'The reason I ask is that you've previously visited your doctor with symptoms of blurred vision and headaches,' Dr Weal says. 'Those things, along with dizziness and fainting, can all be attributed to diabetes.'

I squeeze Mum's hand.

'Nonsense,' Yiayia says. 'I am just getting old. I'm seventy-eight, you know.'

Doctor Weal opens her desk drawer and takes out a flyer titled 'Understanding Diabetes'. 'You're right, in that the risk of diabetes increases over the age of fifty-five,' she says. 'But there are other risk factors such as lack of exercise or poor diet.'

Yiayia shoots me a 'keep quiet' look. She knows I've seen her eating a few too many doughnuts lately.

'I'd like you to have a blood test,' Dr Weal says. 'We can do it here today.'

Yiayia rolls up a sleeve of her cardigan. 'Let's get it over with, then,' she says. 'Then you can cure me.'

'Well, that's the unfortunate thing, Mrs Petropoulos,' Dr Weal says. 'While diabetes can be managed, there is no cure.'

Yiayia's face lights up. 'Wonderful,' she says. 'Chloe, this is a science project for you. Find a cure for diabetes.'

I can't help but laugh.

I wonder what the anti-princesses would say if I proposed a mission to find a cure for a chronic disease that kills millions of people across the world.

CHAPTER SEVENTEEN

Grace is armed with a can of spray paint.

Kailani, Taylor, Ash and Tex have brought along a giant sheet of steel for Grace to attack. Bella, Emily and I are sitting on the grass eating ice-creams and watching them think up a surfers' code of conduct.

A little part of me still doesn't trust the local kids. I want to make sure they don't revert to jerk-mode with Grace – not that she needs rescuing.

'So, I'm going to spray the rules on the sign,' Grace says. 'Then we'll stick it up at the most popular entrance to the main beach – okay?'

Everyone approves.

'I think the first rule should be no tourists,' Taylor says. 'Locals only.'

Grace must feel like she's fighting a losing battle. 'Thanks for the suggestion, Taylor. But isn't the idea to help people get along in the water?'

'Grace is right,' Kailani says, spitting some chewing gum on the ground. 'We should definitely put something about not dropping in.'

'That's the perfect rule, Kailani.' Grace sprays **Surfers' Code of Conduct:** at the top of the sign, followed by

1. Don't drop in. 'What next?'

Ash speaks up. 'Sometimes people get in my way when they're paddling out. It sucks, because I have to flick off my waves.'

Grace nods enthusiastically. 'I hate that too,' she says. 'You need to stay away from the impact zone when you're heading out.'

2. Paddle wide.

Tex high-fives his friend. 'I get angry when I

can't figure out what kooks are doing,' he adds. 'Like when they go right on a wave and I think they're going to go left.'

3. Communicate.

'Very succinct, Grace,' I say. 'Good job.'

Taylor doesn't like me butting in. She throws a pebble in my direction.

'Hey, that was uncalled for,' Grace says. 'But you just reminded me of what I wanted to put down for the next rule.'

4. Don't throw your board.

Kailani claps her hands. 'That's the best one so far. I've crashed into so many runaway boards because people don't hold on to them properly.'

'I have one last suggestion,' Grace says. 'But I'm not sure how to word it.'

Kailani picks up the gum she spat out earlier and throws it into a nearby bin.

'That's it, Kailani!' Grace squeals. 'I think we need to put something down about not littering...but broader than that.'

Kailani takes the spray can from Grace and adds the final point: **5. Show respect.** Then she tosses the empty can into the bin. 'Respect the town, respect the beach, respect each other.'

Grace leaps onto Kailani and gives her a huge hug. Kailani smiles awkwardly. I don't think The Palms kids are big huggers.

'Our surfers' code of conduct is finished!' Grace declares. 'Let's stick it up for everyone to see!'

Tex, Ash, Kailani and Taylor each grab a corner of the sign and follow Grace up the beach.

'You think we can leave them alone with her now?' Bella asks.

I think we can. I think they might even be friends.

Mission Grommet: complete.

CHAPTER EIGHTEEN

We all take turns pushing Bella's billycart up the hill to where drivers register for the derby.

'Are you really sure you'll be okay with no brakes, Bella?' I ask. 'This hill is very steep.'

'The steeper the better,' Bella says. 'I'll go faster.'

There are at least thirty billycarts at the top of the hill: fibreglass ones that look like professional grand prix racers, a couple of converted skateboards, a bathtub on wheels, and something I could've sworn was an aeroplane if it wasn't so small.

'Wow, there are some creative designs here,'

Bella says. 'Mine feels so ordinary.'

Emily runs her hands over the frame of Bella's billycart. 'Don't be like that, Bella,' she says. 'You did an amazing job building this thing in the time you had.'

A man carrying a clipboard strolls over in our direction.

'Urgh, it's Jim the mechanic,' Bella whispers. 'He must be one of the race officials.'

Jim has to look twice to believe it's us. 'Hello there, girls,' he says. 'I see you got your dad to cobble something together for you.'

I think I see a little steam escaping from Bella's ears. 'No one's dad built anything,' she says. 'I made this billycart myself.'

Jim crouches down and examines the cart, tugs the rope and spins the wheels. 'Whoever made it doesn't really matter,' he says. 'It passes the safety test.'

Emily, Grace and I jump up and down.

'Settle down there,' Jim says. 'I need the name of the cart so I can sign you up.'

'It, um, it's called, uh…' Bella stutters.

Jim starts to move to the next cart in line.

'It's called Joan!' Bella shouts. 'Joan of Arc.'

Emily looks concerned as she counts the other drivers. 'It won't be safe if you're all racing down that hill together, Bella.'

Bella straps on her helmet. 'We don't all race together, silly – we race four at a time and a timekeeper records our speeds. They figure out the overall winner at the end.'

'So when is your turn?' Emily asks, relieved.

Jim overhears. 'She's in the first run. You've got five minutes before you're off.'

'Oh no!' Grace says. 'We won't make it down to the bottom of the hill in time.'

'I guess we can watch you from the top, Bella,' I say. 'Let us help you to the start.'

We push Joan of Arc to some makeshift gates. A woman wearing a badge that reads 'Race Marshall' asks who we are.

'I'm Bella Singh,' Bella says. 'And this is my billycart, Joan of Arc.'

The marshall guides Bella towards the second of four gates. There are drivers lined up in the other three spots. Two of the billycarts are similar to Bella's, but the third looks like a rocket ship with its pointy nose and winged rear.

'No pedalling, pushing, paddling or propulsion allowed,' the marshall says. 'And if you crash on the way down, you're disqualified.'

Another official blows a whistle and yells: 'Ready?'

I bend in close so Bella can hear me through her helmet. 'Go, Bella. And be safe.'

Phweeeeeeeeet. Four officials open the four gates and the billycarts roll forward. The crowd begins to cheer.

The carts start slowly. The fancy rocket ship look-alike is immediately a nose ahead.

Bella rocks her body back and forth to get some momentum. I find myself unconsciously mimicking, willing her along, until I realise and force myself to stand still.

'Look at the sidelines,' Emily says. 'There

are hundreds of people here.'

The cheers get louder as the carts get faster. Joan of Arc edges ahead of the pack.

'She's winning!' Grace yells.

One of the carts veers sideways and crashes into a fire hydrant. The driver is a girl about our age. She rubs her knee as she stands up, but she doesn't seem to be seriously injured as she drags her cart off the road.

With just a few metres to go, the rocket is neck-and-neck with Joan of Arc.

'Oh no,' Emily says. 'That rocket thing is going to beat her.'

An official flourishes a chequered flag as the rocket crosses the line just centimetres ahead of Joan of Arc.

I clutch Emily's forearm, accidentally digging my fingernails in.

'I think second place is the least of our worries,' I say. 'Bella can't stop.'

Grace sprints off down the hill. Emily and I aren't far behind, frantically parting the crowd to get through.

'She mustn't have brakes,' a girl says.

'She's crashed!' says a woman.

I jump and try to see. The crowd is too thick and I'm too short.

'Coming through!' Emily screams.

We finally reach the finish line, where we find Joan of Arc upside down and wedged between some hay bales.

Grace gets there first and helps some officials pull Bella out of the cart.

'Bella, are you okay?' I ask, crouching down to her level. I'm expecting blood. Or at least tears.

Bella slips off her helmet, revealing a huge smile. 'That was amazing,' she says. 'Can I do it again?'

Mission Revhead: complete.

CHAPTER NINETEEN

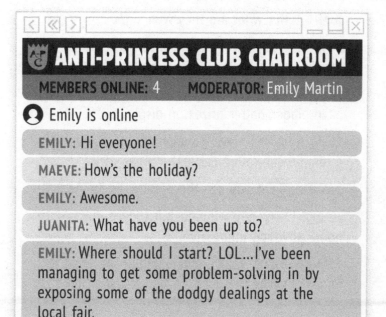

ANTI-PRINCESS CLUB CHATROOM

MEMBERS ONLINE: 4   **MODERATOR:** Emily Martin

Emily is online

EMILY: Hi everyone!

MAEVE: How's the holiday?

EMILY: Awesome.

JUANITA: What have you been up to?

EMILY: Where should I start? LOL...I've been managing to get some problem-solving in by exposing some of the dodgy dealings at the local fair.

LEAH: I've always wondered why I never win anything at carnivals.

EMILY: Has anyone ever played that game where you fish a rubber duck out of the pond?

MAEVE: Yes – they have numbers on the bottom of the ducks that match a bunch of different prizes.

EMILY: That's the one. But I'm a little stuck at trying to work out if it's crooked like the others. So far, everyone I've seen play has won something.

JUANITA: But what are they winning?

EMILY: Oh, you know, little things like bracelets, pencils, stickers.

LEAH: So they're winning crummy prizes? Do they have bigger, better prizes on display?

EMILY: Yes. They have a bunch of cool things like a remote-controlled car and a pogo stick.

JUANITA: Don't you see the pattern, Emily?

MAEVE: Everyone's winning, but they're not taking home anything impressive.

JUANITA: That's your problem, Emily. You need to figure out why the good prizes are gathering dust.

Emily slaps her laptop shut. 'It's so simple!' she says. 'I was overthinking it, but I've finally figured out the truth behind the duck pond. We've got to get back to the fair.'

'Dad!' I yell. 'We need you to take us to the showground, fast! And please!'

'Why are you girls so desperate to get to the fair?' Dad asks, grabbing his keys. 'Is it one of your princess club missions?'

'It's *anti*-princess club, Dad,' I say. 'And, yes, we do have a mission to complete.'

I jump in the front passenger seat as the other anti-princesses pile into the back of the van.

'So, tell me,' Dad says as he starts the engine.

'I'm bringing down the sideshow alley, Mr Karalis,' Emily says. 'I'm unveiling the secrets behind the carnies' games and unmasking them as the fraudsters they really are.'

Dad makes a 'hmmmm' sound as he takes a left turn. 'You know, girls,' he says, 'it's a hard life these carnival folk lead. They rely on those few dollars you hand over for a game to make their living. And I don't think they like being called "carnies", either. "Stallholders" is a much nicer word.'

'Why is he defending them?' Emily mumbles in the back. 'They're criminals.'

Dad and I overhear. 'I admire your ethics,' he says. 'They might *technically* be criminals, but they're hardly comparable to big-time thieves. Just have a think about whether they're causing more harm than fun.'

Dad has a point. The anti-princesses could be ruining the livelihoods of entire families, and I guess fairs wouldn't exist without them.

We get out of the van and I kiss Dad goodbye. 'Thanks, Dad,' I say. 'We'll remember what you said.'

Emily's not in so much of a rush to get to the duck pond now. She strolls through the sideshow alley with the stallholders watching her warily. 'It does look a little less crowded today,' she says. 'Do you think it's my fault?'

No one quite knows the answer.

'You again,' the stallholder says when we get to the duck pond.

Emily leans in close and speaks quietly. 'If I pulled all of those ducks out of the pond and arranged them by number, what would I find?'

His gaze shifts sideways.

Emily answers for him. 'Every number under those ducks corresponds with a cheap prize, doesn't it? It's impossible to win the fancy prizes, because you haven't marked any ducks with the numbers that match them.'

He grunts and kicks the base of the plastic pond.

'Here's the deal,' Emily says. 'I won't make a fuss and call you out public if you compromise with me.'

The stallholder reaches into his canvas bag and extends a handful of money to Emily. 'You win. How much do you want?'

Emily pushes his hand away. 'I don't want to be paid,' she says. 'I want you to take two of the good prizes down and put them away. Then, grab one duck out of the pond and write the number of the remaining good prize on that duck.'

The stallholder takes the pogo stick and the doll down from his display. Then he takes a duck and writes '18' on the bottom – the same number as on the remote-controlled car left on his shelf.

'Now you've got forty-five ducks in that pond and just one good prize on offer,' Emily says. 'They're still great odds for you. Who knows, you might even get to keep the car at the end of the day.' She hands him two dollars. 'I'll be your first customer now that the game's fair.'

The stallholder's eyes soften as he passes Emily a hook. She reaches into the pond and pulls out a duck. 'Number 26.'

He shrugs sheepishly and offers Emily a striped pencil.

'No, thanks,' she says. 'Just don't underestimate the brains of the kids at your next fair.'

The carnie takes off his cap and rubs the top of his head. He stares at us, dumbfounded, as we walk away.

'I'm proud of you, Emily,' I say. 'You exposed the tricksters, but this time you were fair about it.'

Mission ~~Carnie~~ Stallholder Cracker: complete.

CHAPTER  TWENTY

I can't believe our holiday is almost over.

Part of me wants to get home to my telescope. As well as my microscope. And my stethoscope. All of my things ending in 'scope,' really.

But another part wants to stay here eating doughnuts for breakfast and watching the sunrise with the anti-princesses.

I sit up in bed and see Grace stretching quietly on the floor while Bella and Emily sleep.

'Good morning,' Grace whispers. 'I think the whole house is still snoozing.'

That's strange. Yiayia is usually up before everyone and has at least a pot of chamomile tea brewing.

I step out of bed into my slippers and shuffle into the kitchen. It's cold and empty.

I tiptoe down the hall to Yiayia's bedroom and push the door open. 'Yiayia? Wakey, wakey.'

But Yiayia's not there. She must have woken extra early so she could enjoy her final proper morning on holiday. Tomorrow we'll be packing up and leaving straight after breakfast.

I walk to the back door. A gust of wind makes me shiver as I step onto the deck.

'Yiayia?' I call. 'Are you there? Yiayia! Where are you?'

'What's wrong, Chloe?' Mum asks, appearing at the door with Alex behind her. 'What are you yelling about?'

'I can't find Yiayia.' My voice shakes.

Mum goes into leader mode. She's always been good at keeping calm and delegating.

I notice it the most when she's in the restaurant – she's an amazing maître d'.

'Alex, check all the rooms inside and then look around the yard,' she says. 'Chloe, you and the girls do a quick run to the beach, but come straight back. Your dad and I will go for a little drive around the block. We might spot Yiayia from the van.'

I'm so focused on finding Yiayia, I don't bother changing my slippers to proper shoes. I don't even realise Grace, Bella and Emily are puffing along behind me until we get to the path through the dunes.

We all stop when we reach the empty beach.

'Yiayia?' I scream. 'Yiayia!'

Emily puts her arm around me. 'I'm sure she's fine, wherever she is. Don't get too worked up, Chloe.'

'I think Yiayia might be really sick,' I sob. 'The doctor thinks she could have diabetes. I wanted to wait until the test results were in before I told you.'

Grace tries to be the voice of reason. 'Let's not jump to conclusions. We're assuming the worst too soon.'

I sprint to the water and scan the shoreline as far as I can see. Grace checks the dunes near the beach path, while Emily and Bella run up and down the sand.

'Let's go back!' I call. 'She might have turned up already.'

We all run back to the house and see Mum, Dad and Alex at the front door.

'Was there no sign of her at the beach?' Dad asks. Alex and Mum look to us hopefully.

'No,' I say. 'There was no one down there at all.'

Alex starts to cry. He doesn't show his emotions very often. He must be really scared.

'We'll take the van out again – you can come with us, Alex,' Mum says. 'An extra pair of eyes could help.'

I open the van door and Mum shakes her head. 'No, Chloe,' she says. 'Stay here with the girls in case Yiayia comes back.'

As the van reverses out of the driveway, I sob uncontrollably. Emily, Bella and Grace put their arms around me.

'Let's boil the kettle,' Bella says. 'We'll have some tea waiting for Yiayia.'

'I propose a mission,' I say, wiping my nose on my sleeve. 'Mission Yiayia: find my grand-mother.'

Emily, Grace and Bella hold hands and raise their arms together.

'Of course we're all in favour,' Emily says. 'It's our most important mission yet.'

I hope it's a mission we don't actually have to complete. I hope Yiayia comes home on her own, safe and sound.

CHAPTER
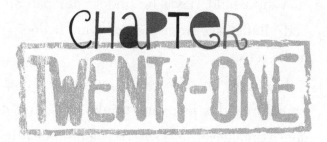
TWENTY-ONE

Mission Yiayia.

The words on Emily's laptop screen seem surreal.

The one person who's never far from my side has disappeared into thin air.

'I'm going to do another whip around the beach,' Grace says. 'Just to be sure.'

I decide to take an umpteenth trawl around the inside of the house.

I open a cupboard in the hallway – nothing but spare sheets and pillowcases. I look in the pantry – nothing but jars, bags and boxes of food. I peer under Mum and Dad's bed –

nothing but a pair of shoes and a book.

'Why would Yiayia be under your parents' bed?' Bella asks from the doorway. 'It doesn't make sense.'

I take off my glasses and rub my temples. Sometimes this helps me think. 'Of course it doesn't make sense,' I say. 'Yiayia disappearing doesn't make sense either.'

Having a scientific brain means I sometimes struggle with mystery. I believe there's an explanation for everything, and when an answer isn't obvious I can't rest until I figure out the truth.

Emily knocks on the door. 'Grace is talking to the surfer kids out there,' she says. 'I think they might have some info about Yiayia.'

I yank the window shutters open and see Grace standing with Kailani, Taylor, Ash and Tex. 'Have you seen Yiayia?' I call out to them.

'A little old lady with grey hair?' Kailani calls back. 'And a purple robe?'

That's Yiayia and her fluffy purple dressing

gown. It has tiny violets on it
if you look closely. Violets are
the national flower of Greece.

I burst through the back
door and jump down all six
steps between the deck and
the lawn.

'They saw Yiayia this morning,'
Grace says. 'Tell her, Kailani.'

Our van pulls up in the driveway and
Mum leaps out. The panic has finally set in
for her. 'We couldn't see her anywhere. I'm
going to call the police.'

'Wait,' I say. 'These kids say they saw Yiayia
earlier.'

Mum, Dad and Alex bombard Kailani,
Taylor, Ash and Tex with questions.

'Where was she?'

'When did you see her?'

'Are you sure it was her?'

Kailani picks up her surfboard and holds it
in front of herself like a shield. 'Slow down!

I'll answer all your questions,' she says. 'We saw her walking up the beach this morning.'

I don't understand why Yiayia would've been on the beach without me. 'What time?' I ask.

Kailani spits on her watch and rubs its face with her sleeve. 'It's nine o'clock now, so I'd say it was about half past five.'

Mum isn't buying Kailani's story. 'Aren't you the kids who were picking on Grace when we arrived?'

I pull Mum aside. 'We settled things,' I say. 'You can trust them.'

Taylor steps in to defend her friend. 'Look,' she says, 'we were out for a super early surf. There's no tourists in the water at that time. And we saw her walking along the sand.'

Grace is bouncing from foot to foot, ready to launch into an Olympic-speed sprint along the beach in search of Yiayia.

'She was heading north,' Taylor continues. 'We lost sight of her around the main beach entrance. You know, where we stuck the surfers' code of conduct.'

Grace is off.

'Thank you,' I say. 'We're supposed to be heading home tomorrow, so if we don't see you around I guess we'll catch up next time we're in town.'

Kailani jumps in front of me and I almost dart away until I realise she wants a hug. I open my arms and accept her embrace.

'I hope you find your grandma,' Kailani says into my hair. 'And we'll see you next holidays.'

Bella and Emily are the next to cop cuddles. It's all very sweet, except I don't have time to be mushy. I need to find Yiayia. I run along Grace's track of footprints in the sand.

Before the voices of the local kids fade in the distance I hear Tex yell, 'Tell Grace she can surf all right!'

I guess that's a compliment.

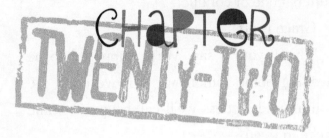

CHAPTER TWENTY-TWO

'Yiayia!'

'Yiayia, are you there?'

'Yiayia, where are you?!'

The anti-princesses, as well as Mum, Dad and Alex, are pacing around the beach track where the local kids last saw Yiayia.

The shouting is useless. Even if she was here earlier, she's not here anymore.

'If Yiayia's fallen ill somewhere, time is racing against us,' Mum says. 'I'm calling the police and heading back to the house – someone should be there.'

Dad yells out for Yiayia one last time. His

voice echoes into nothingness. 'I'll come with you,' he says to Mum.

Alex is hesitant to leave. 'I might hang around just a bit longer. If she really was here, she might come back.'

Bella, Emily and Grace turn to me for guidance. 'What do you want to do, Chloe?' Bella asks. 'Should we go back with your mum and dad?'

We've already combed the beach between our holiday house and the surfers' code of conduct sign. We need to go somewhere new.

'I don't think we should go back along the sand,' I say. 'Let's go into town. It's just a few blocks. Yiayia might have had the urge to do some window shopping or something equally ridiculous.'

Mum and Dad have already left, so I can't ask their permission. They've let us walk into town on our own before, so long as we stay together as a group.

'Alex, I promise we'll be back in under an

hour,' I say. 'Tell Mum and Dad, okay?'

He nods. Alex knows he can trust me.

The anti-princesses and I link arms and walk past rows of beach houses along the road leading into the main street. We stop outside a hair salon called Crops and Bobbers. I'd laugh at the clever name if I wasn't so worried about Yiayia.

'Eight shops on each side on the road,' Emily says. 'Let's pop into four shops each and ask if they've seen Yiayia.'

I knew I could rely on her for mathematical logic. 'Good plan. Let's meet at the general store up the end,' I say. 'No one move from there once you're done. We don't want to lose another person.'

I open the sliding door of Crops and Bobbers. 'Excuse me,' I say. 'Have you seen an older lady with grey hair this morning, possibly wearing a purple dressing gown?'

A man with a comb between his teeth laughs. 'We see plenty of grey hair here,' he says. 'But no purple dressing gown today, sorry. We've only been open a few minutes, mind you – don't usually open at all on Sundays but we thought we'd make the most of the tourist trade. You need an appointment?'

I shake my head and run next door to the seafood shop. The smell of raw fish hits my nostrils as I pop my head in. 'I'm looking for my grandmother,' I say. 'She's short, grey-haired, and was wearing a purple dressing gown this morning. Have you seen her?'

The dead fish look more lively than the fishmongers, who stare at me blankly.

I have no more luck in the bakery, and the real estate agent's office is closed, so I make my way to the general store where I find Grace and Emily waiting.

'No sightings here at the general store or either of the cafes, and the gift shop was shut,' Grace says.

Emily is also the bearer of bad news. 'Nothing from the bait-and-tackle shop, the newsagent or the burger place – and the solicitor's office was closed.'

Bella's last to arrive and I can tell by her mopey expression that she failed too. 'Sorry, Chloe,' she says. 'Ralph and Jim's garages were both locked up.'

I fight the urge to cry again. Tears aren't going to be any help right now. 'I guess we should just head home,' I say. 'Let's see what the police say.'

We link arms and march off once more. Worst-case scenarios are starting to swirl through my head, so I whistle to distract myself.

Yap, yap, yap. Yap. Yap. It's the dog we met

the other day. My whistling set it off.

'How did your billycart go?' a voice calls out.

Joan of Arc is sitting on her front porch, a teapot and two cups on an upside-down milk crate next to her rocking chair.

'Oh, great, thank you,' Bella says. 'I couldn't have done it without all your wonderful donations.'

Joan slowly steps down onto her path. I know she's feeble, but I wish she'd hurry up. We are in the middle of an emergency mission, after all.

She reaches the gate and extends her hand to Bella. 'Congratulations on finishing the race,' she says. 'Back in my day, you wouldn't have caught a girl racing a billycart. Or, rather, we wouldn't have been allowed to.'

Bella shakes Joan's hand. 'Thank you again,' she says. 'But we really must be going now.'

Joan nods and turns back to her porch. 'I'd love to see the billycart some time. I think that's only fair, seeing I'm its namesake.'

'Of course,' Bella calls out, and we hurry away before we get caught up in small talk for any longer.

Thirty seconds down the road Bella grinds to a halt. 'Wait!' she yells. 'How did Joan know we named the billycart after her?'

'Who cares right now?' I ask.

'Trust me.' Bella tugs me back towards Joan's house. 'I think I'm onto something here.'

Yap, yap, yap. Yap. Yap.

'You're back,' Joan calls from her rocking chair. 'Did you drop something?'

Bella risks a nip and pats the dog to stop its yapping. 'Joan, how did you know I named the billycart after you?'

Joan picks up one of the teacups and takes a sip. 'Your grandmother told me. She stopped to pat Maggie when she was on her walk this morning and I invited her up for a cup of tea.'

'That's my yiayia!' I say. 'We've lost her. What time did you last see her?'

'Let me think.' Joan takes another sip of tea.

'She was here for a long while having a good old natter about you girls. She left around two hours ago.'

Emily frowns as she figures it out. 'Let's say Yiayia left here around seven-thirty,' she says. 'Even at her pace, she should've been back ages ago.'

'Maybe Yiayia didn't go straight home. Which way did she go when she left here?' I ask Joan.

Joan leans forward and peers down the road. 'She veered left past the park towards the fairground. The fair's in town, you know.'

Bella climbs the gate and jumps onto the porch. She kisses Joan on the cheek. 'Thanks again, Joan,' she says. 'You really are a saviour.'

We don't even need to consult each other on our next move.

To the fairground it is.

CHAPTER TWENTY-THREE

It's the final day of the fair, which means almost the entire population of The Palms has decided to come along.

It's chaos, even for a town of only seven hundred people plus tourists.

'What now?' Grace asks. 'Do you really think she's here?'

The crowd is distracting me.

'Chloe!' Bella, Emily and Grace scream my name at once.

I've fallen onto the ground. No. Something pushed me onto the ground. I lift my head and realise I'm nose-to-snout with a pig.

'Sorry about that,' a boy in a straw hat says. 'I'm trying to get Josie here to the arena for her race, but she pulled away from me because she could smell cake.'

'Um, no problem,' I say as Grace helps me up. 'I run into cake-eating pigs all the time.' What else is there to say after being bowled over by a pig?

As I watch the boy jog off with Josie, I smell cake too. My mind drifts back to being on the deck with Emily, swinging in the hammock, talking with Yiayia about the fair.

'Cake!' I say.

'I don't think we can stop for cake right now, Chloe,' Emily says. 'We need to find Yiayia.'

I close my eyes and think harder. 'Yiayia wanted to see the cake display at the fair!'

Emily's eyes light up as the memory registers for her too. 'When we were reading the newspaper, Yiayia specifically said, "Cake display – I would like to see that."'

We hold hands and run through the masses of people milling in the sideshow alley.

I'm not sure we know exactly where we're going. Emily has the same realisation and stops at the duck pond.

The stallholder holds up his hands defensively. 'Look, little lady, there's nothing shady going on here. I took your advice and made sure—'

'I just need to know where the cake display is,' Emily interrupts. 'Can you tell me?'

The stallholder's relieved. 'In the pavilion,' he says, pointing to the other side of the arena. 'Better be quick – the cakes are all on sale now because it's the last day of the fair.'

We race to the pavilion and burst through the doors.

The smell of sugar hits my nose. There are sweets everywhere – cakes, biscuits, pastries. I scan the rows of treats, wondering what would have drawn Yiayia in.

'There!' I yell. 'Baklava!'

We mob the man standing behind the pastries.

'Have you seen a lady in a purple dressing gown?' Emily asks.

The man strokes his beard as he thinks. He looks just like my dad. I wonder if he's Greek too.

'*Kalimera*,' I say. 'I'm looking for my yiayia.'

Kalimera means 'good morning' in Greek.

'*Kalimera sas*,' he says. 'Please taste my baklava. It has your yiayia's approval.'

The anti-princesses squeal and jump on the spot.

'So she was here!' I ask. 'Did you speak to her?'

The man pushes his plate closer to my face. I take a piece of baklava and gobble it down to keep him happy.

'Yes, she was the first one here this morning,' he says. 'How could I forget a woman from my homeland?' The man rubs his thumb and forefingers together. He wants money.

'Did she tell you her plans?' I ask. 'Or where she was going next?'

Emily throws a handful of change at the man in exchange for a bag of baklava.

'Thank you for your business,' he says. 'What was your verdict on my sample?'

His recipe doesn't come close to being as good as mine, but there's no time to give him pointers. I tell a white lie. 'It's delicious,' I say. 'Now what about Yiayia?'

He strokes his beard again. 'Ah, we spoke about Hydra and how she used to holiday there as a child. She told me she loved Pacific Palms too and that her favourite place was the lake. She was on her way to the lake.'

The lake. Of course. Our special place.

Our holiday is almost over and I haven't been to the lake with Yiayia.

I've been so busy with my friends that I've neglected my grandmother. She wanted to feed the seagulls so badly that she went alone.

It's all my fault.

CHAPTER TWENTY-FOUR

The forest along the track to the lake is a lot thicker than I remember. I guess that's what happens when you only visit once or twice a year.

A twig scratches my face as I run along the narrow dirt pathway, but I don't care. I just need to get to Yiayia.

I sent Bella and Grace back to the holiday house to tell Mum, Dad and Alex where Emily and I were going. They shouldn't be far away. The lake is only about a ten-minute walk from everywhere at The Palms.

'Why didn't we come here earlier?' Emily

asks. 'I mean, it sounds like it's an important place to you and Yiayia.'

'I *should*'ve come earlier,' I say, slapping a mosquito as it lands on my cheek. 'I guess I got sidetracked with the fair and the surfing and the billycart derby.'

Emily's bottom lip drops. I realise I've just blamed the anti-princesses for stopping us coming to the lake.

'It's not your fault,' I say. 'Yiayia got sick too. Every time we planned to come here, she seemed to collapse or hurt herself.'

We round a bend and stop suddenly. A torrent of water is running across the track up ahead.

'That doesn't look like a lake,' Emily says. 'It's more of a river.'

I cautiously walk closer to the water. I dip my finger in and taste it. 'That's sea water. The tide must be coming in.' I need to see past the river to get my bearings. 'Can you give me a boost up into this tree?' I ask Emily.

She links her fingers and I stand on her

hands, grab the lowest limb of the tree and pull myself onto it.

There's a blur of blue in the distance. It's the lake. And in between there's a strip of land, like a mini-island.

'What can you see?' Emily asks.

I push some pine needles out of the way.

There she is! She's lying down. Surrounded by seagulls. 'Yiayia!' I scream. 'I see her!'

Yiayia doesn't answer or move.

'Please let her be sleeping. Please, please, please,' I whisper.

'We've found her!' Emily yells.

She's talking to Bella and Grace. They've just turned up, dragging the billycart behind them.

'Where's Mum and Dad?' I ask. 'And Alex?'

'They weren't there,' Grace says, helping me down from the tree. 'We had to leave a note.'

Without thinking, I run to the water. Grace and Emily grab an arm each and wrench me back. 'You don't know how deep it is,' Grace says. 'Or how strong the current is.'

The clang of metal jolts me to my senses. Bella is tinkering with the billycart.

'What is that doing here?' I ask. 'And what are you doing with it?'

Bella pulls one of the wheels off its axle. 'We thought it would get us here quicker than running,' she says. 'And now I'm turning it into a raft.'

My heart is pounding and my breath is shortening. I feel like I'm going to spew. They're all classic symptoms of stress overload. It's Biology 101.

'Will it float?' Emily asks.

'It's just a timber frame,' Bella says. 'It will be light enough without wheels and axles.' She kicks the driver's seat.

'What are you doing now?' I ask.

The plastic chair tumbles off as Bella kicks it a second time.

'I have to make enough room for two people to lie down on this thing,' she says. 'Grace is going to paddle Yiayia across the water.'

Grace is a little stunned. 'You want me to paddle it?' she asks. 'Like a surfboard?'

'It's either that or wait for the tide to go down,' Bella says, carrying the raft to the water. 'Emily, when will that be?'

'The time between two high tides is twelve hours and twenty-five minutes.' Emily looks at her watch. 'Yiayia was on the beach at six, Joan's house at seven-thirty and the cake display at eight. So, she would've made it here before nine and the river must have been a dry bed or very shallow for her to cross. It's eleven now, so by my calculations the tide is going to get higher before it gets lower. Low tide won't be here again until around nine tonight.'

Grace flicks off her shoes and rolls up her pants. 'Well, we don't have time to wait for the water to recede,' she says 'We don't even have time to go and get help in town. We need to rescue Yiayia ourselves.'

Bella holds the raft steady while Grace lies on top belly-down and shuffles to the front.

She dangles her arms into the water and starts to paddle, just like she does on her surfboard.

'Let's go,' Grace says.

Bella launches Grace into the river. The momentum from the push has the raft halfway there. Now it's up to Grace and her muscles to get the rest of the way to Yiayia.

'You can do it, Grace!' I yell.

Grace is paddling hard. 'The current's not too strong!' she calls. 'Just a few more strokes!'

I climb back up the pine tree so I can see Grace and Yiayia. *Thump*. The front of the raft hits land and we all squeal.

Grace jumps off and drags it out of the water. 'Yiayia!' she calls. 'It's me, Grace! I'm here!' She puts her ear up against Yiayia's chest. 'She's breathing!'

I cross my fingers in hope that Yiayia has just fainted again. Maybe she was light-headed after walking so far on her own.

'She won't wake up!' Grace yells.

Bella and Emily are waiting for instructions

from me, but I don't know where I fit. Bella used her awesome talent to knock together the raft, Emily figured out the timing of the tides with her maths skills, and Grace's strength got the raft across the water. I feel so helpless.

'I don't know what to do,' I say.

Emily calls out to Grace. 'You have to get Yiayia on the raft!' she calls. 'Unconscious or not!'

Grace hooks her elbows through Yiayia's armpits and drags her across the ground. She slides her onto the raft and moves her body into the middle of the wooden frame.

'Be careful, Grace!' I yell.

Grace slowly pushes the raft into the water and climbs on. This time, instead of lying down, she kneels.

'Can you paddle like that?' Bella asks.

Grace leans forward and pulls at the water with her hands. It looks tougher this way, and the added weight from Yiayia is only making it worse. 'Don't worry!' Grace shouts. 'I've seen lifesavers do this on surf skis!'

The raft is halfway across when Grace starts to lose balance. It wobbles as she falls forward onto her chest.

Bella and Emily scream and I turn away. I whisper to myself, 'Not much further. Not much further.'

I jump down from the tree so I have a better view of the river.

Grace is back on her knees, paddling like some sort of super duck. 'We're okay!' she yells. 'Just a little further!'

I take one step into the water. The raft is so close, I can almost reach it.

'Branch!' Emily screams. 'Watch out!'

A tree branch appears out of nowhere between me and the raft.

Grace tries to steer around it, but accidentally spins the raft back towards the island. As she tries to correct the direction, she slips clean off and into the stream.

'Grace!' Bella screams.

Grace's head pops out of the water. 'I can

touch the bottom! It's okay!'

Bella, Emily and I run into the river and grab the raft. We heave it towards us, but the sudden jerk sends Yiayia sliding off the edge.

All four anti-princesses lunge to lift her above the water. She was only under for a second or two.

I cradle her head while Emily, Bella and Grace grab her arms and legs and carry her to land. We lay her down and I roll her onto her side. I open her mouth to check her airways.

Cough, cough, cough. Cough, cough, cough.

'Yiayia,' I say. 'It's Chloe. Can you hear me?'

The shock from the dip in the stream has helped liven her up, but she still can't speak or open her eyes fully. This is more than light-headedness. It's got to be the diabetes.

I think back to the information Dr Weal gave us. 'Hypoglycaemia,' I say. 'It's hypoglycaemia!'

Now it's the other anti-princesses looking helpless.

'What can we do?' Emily asks.

Food. Yiayia needs food. A carbohydrate. Something sugary. Something…

'Emily, I need your baklava,' I say. 'Quickly.'

She doesn't understand my request, but she hands over her bag of pastries in a flash.

I rub the baklava on Yiayia's lips. 'Hypoglycaemia is something that happens to diabetics when their blood glucose gets too low,' I say. 'It can happen when you haven't eaten enough or you've exercised too much.'

Yiayia starts to lick her lips. I hold the baklava steady as she takes a nibble. 'That's it, Yiayia,' I say. 'Eat up.'

Her nibbling grows to proper chewing. Her chewing grows to proper eating.

Yiayia reaches up and snatches the bag of baklava from my hands.

She opens her eyes and grins cheekily. 'That's not your baklava, Chloe,' she says. 'Yours is much better.'

I wrap my arms around her.

'Chloe! Yiayia!'

It's Mum, Dad and Alex calling through the trees. They must have got the note.

'I'm sorry, girls,' Yiayia says. 'You must be disappointed in me.'

Emily, Grace and Bella join Yiayia and me in a giant group bear hug.

'We're not disappointed, Yiayia,' I say. 'Just worried.'

Yiayia sighs. 'I am not an anti-princess after all,' she says. 'I needed rescuing.'

I kiss her forehead. Over and over again. 'We'll let you off this time,' I say. 'You're okay, and that's a fairytale ending I don't mind.'

Mission Yiayia: complete.

EPILOGUE

Mum, Dad and Alex were at the police station when Grace and Bella turned up at the holiday house. Apparently they couldn't take a missing person's report over the phone.

A paramedic and a police officer arrived at the lake not long after my parents, and they were very impressed by our rescue efforts. The paramedic was especially stoked to hear about the way I handled Yiayia's hypoglycaemia. He said treating someone with low blood sugar could be a complicated science, but I got it just right.

The day after we arrived home, we found

out officially that Yiayia tested positive for Type 2 diabetes. Now that she knows she has it, she can manage it with medication and eating well. And I've made it my life's mission to find a cure for the disease. I thought it was a bit too ambitious when Yiayia first suggested it, but I'm only ten, right? I've got my whole life to complete that mission.

About a week after we got back home to Newcastle, Grace got barrelled. All the surfing practice at The Palms must have helped. I set Dad's camera up on a tripod at the beach and snapped Grace on her board just as she emerged from the tube. We emailed Kailani straightaway. Those kids won't dare call Grace a kook again.

As for the code of conduct, a bunch of pro surfers read it and are now campaigning for all popular breaks along the coast to erect their own signs. They reckon they should've come up with the idea years ago.

On our way home, Mum stopped the van

at Joan of Arc's house so we could thank her again for the billycart materials. Unfortunately, we couldn't show her the cart because we had dismantled it and turned it into a raft. When we told her what had happened she was happy it had played a part in Yiayia's rescue.

As a final way of showing our gratitude, we all chipped in and gave Joan's front yard a quick clean-up. We filled up Dad and Alex's car with junk to take to the dump, but not before Bella claimed a few key pieces for her next project. She says she's going to build a boat. I think she got a taste for water at The Palms.

Word has spread about Emily and her maths sleuthing skills. She found a carnie chatroom that warned fair folk to be on the lookout for a nosy girl with red hair. Emily found it pretty funny, but decided the stallholders were relatively harmless when you put things in perspective. I can see her twenty years from now working as a top detective bringing down internet scammers, and corrupt bankers and stockbrokers. No one will cross her.

I wonder if the anti-princesses will want to come back to The Palms on our next family holiday. I think they will – surely a second trip couldn't be as drama-filled as the first.

Whatever lies ahead, there's one thing I'm certain of: we won't need rescuing.